Big Machines, Cars and Trucks

Written by Marc Cerasini
Illustrated by Mac Cruise

© 1997 McClanahan Book Company, Inc.
All rights reserved.
Published by McClanahan Book Company, Inc.
23 West 26th Street, New York, NY 10010
ISBN 1-56293-905-X
LCC: 96-78357
Printed in the U.S.A.

In the City

    Sirens wail along city streets. Two fire trucks come
racing through the heavy traffic. One is a pumper truck
that holds big tanks of water. Its hoses can pump hundreds
of gallons of water onto a fire. The other is a ladder truck
that carries long ladders to reach the tops of tall buildings.

An ambulance follows, carrying an emergency medical crew and equipment to help people who are sick or hurt. Then it takes them to the hospital. Its loud siren and flashing lights warn other trucks and cars to move out of its way!

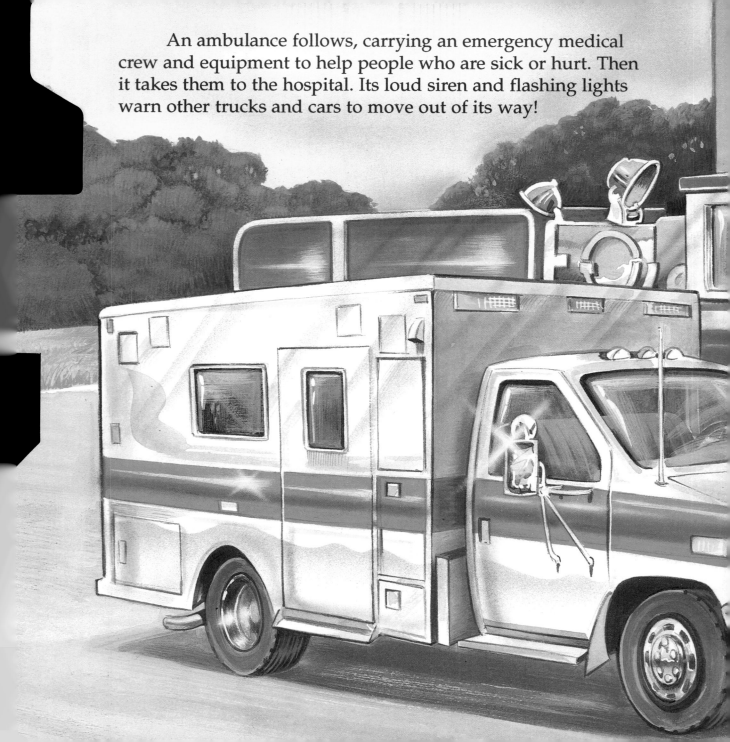

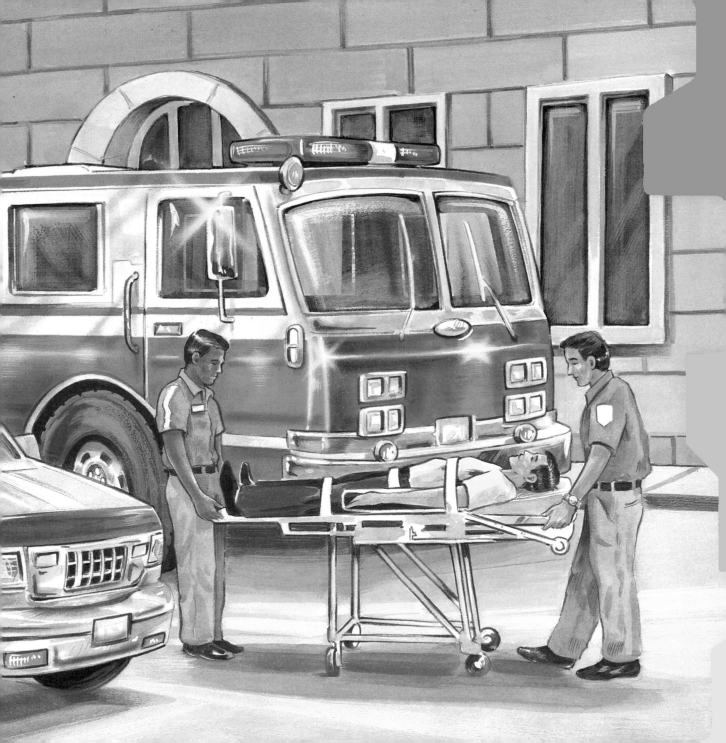

In the Town

Big yellow school buses drive children to and from school. They pass all kinds of cars—sedans, station wagons, sportscars, convertibles—and vans that can carry large families. On the streets, too, are many different kinds of trucks.

Refrigerator trucks keep food cold. Beverage trucks deliver bottles of soda to supermarkets. Other delivery trucks bring food. Ice cream trucks bring treats right to the sidewalk. Postal trucks deliver mail. Garbage trucks collect the trash.

In the Country

On farms, tractors pull plows to till the soil so it is ready
for planting. They also pull machines that plant seeds.

Big trucks called harvesters gather crops when they are ready to be picked.

On the Road

Tanker trucks haul oil, milk, and other liquids. Trucks with large open trailers take new cars from the factory to the showroom. And moving vans carry people's belongings when they move to a new house.

When work needs to be done on telephone poles and high-tension wires, trucks with long cherry pickers lift workers high into the air. The tow truck will hook itself up to a car with engine trouble and take it to a service station to get fixed.

Off the Road

All-terrain vehicles (ATVs) with four-wheel drive can go places other cars can't. They are built high enough to drive through shallow streams and slippery mud.

Monster trucks are made for car-and-truck shows, called rallies. Their giant wheels can roll over almost anything—even other cars!

Dune buggies are built for driving on the beach. They have wide tires that grip the sand. If they should roll over, their special roofs will not get crushed.

Race cars are the fastest cars in the world. They are so fast that they can be driven only on racetracks. Race cars are built by hand, so no two are alike. They are low to the ground and have special shapes so the air doesn't slow them down.

At the Airport

An airport has specially built cars and trucks to service the airplanes. Scissor trucks lift food and cargo into the body of passenger planes. Stair trucks bring steps to the airplane door so people can get off and on. Baggage cars pull two or three carts behind them, filled with luggage.

At the Construction Site

The biggest trucks of all are hard at work on this construction site. A mass excavator has a long arm with a bucket on the end. It digs up dirt and rock and dumps them into a dump truck. This giant dump truck carries tons of dirt and rocks above wheels that are larger than a person.

Bulldozers have a large metal blade in front that pushes dirt or rubble away and leaves the land clear for building.

Cement mixers have a huge barrel that spins around, making concrete to pave road and sidewalks.

Pavers lay the surface for new roads. Rollers follow, smoothing out the surface. Together, they help make it possible for all the cars, trucks, and big machines to get where they are going safely and comfortably.